A Little Princess

based on the story by
Frances Hodgson Burnett

Adapted by
Susanna Davidson

Illustrated by **Kate Aldous**

Reading Consultant: Alison Kelly
Roehampton University

Contents

Chapter 1
Sara

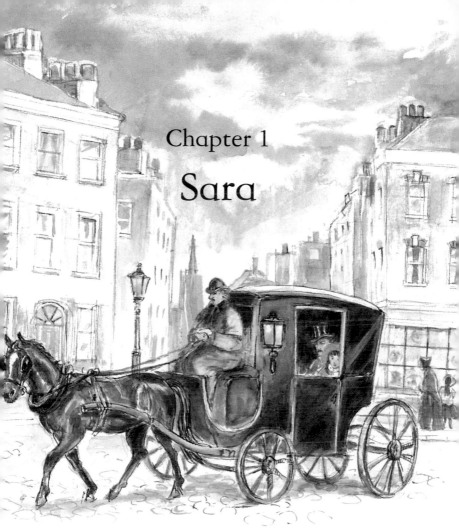

A young girl stared out from a cab at the foggy London streets. Her name was Sara Crewe, and it was her first time in England.

She had come with her father the week before, on a huge ship all the way from India. And tomorrow her father would be sailing back... without her.

The cab stopped by a dull brick house. Outside was a large brass sign that read *Miss Minchin's Boarding School for Young Ladies*.

"Is this the place, Papa?"
Sara asked, hesitantly.

"Yes, this is it," Captain Crewe
replied, squeezing her hand.

Just then, the heavy front door
opened, and Miss Minchin came
out to greet them. She had cold,
fishy eyes, and a cold, fishy smile.

Miss Minchin's
Boarding
School for
Young Ladies

"You must be Sara," she said. "Welcome to your new home. Oh, what a pretty child you are!"

And spoiled, I expect.

Behind Miss Minchin came Miss Amelia, her younger sister.

"Welcome! Welcome!" she said, bobbing up and down with a nervous curtsey.

"Sara is to have everything she wants," said Captain Crewe. "I want no expense spared."

"Of course," said Miss Minchin, a cold smile creeping over her lips. "As our richest pupil, she'll have the prettiest bedroom, a pony and carriage and her very own maid."

Captain Crewe went with Sara to her sitting-room. "I'm sure you'll be happy here," he said. "You couldn't have stayed in India with me. The heat made you ill and the schools are better here..."

"I know," said Sara, trying to be brave. But now the moment had come to say goodbye, it was even more awful than she'd imagined. They hugged each other as if they'd never let go.

Chapter 2

Boarding school

When Sara came down the next morning, everyone stared at her. All the girls had heard that the new pupil was as rich as a princess.

"She's even got a French maid," whispered Jessie, one of the older pupils. "And I saw her trunk. It's full of fur coats."

"Well," Jessie's friend Lavinia added spitefully, "I heard Miss Minchin say her clothes were ridiculously grand for a child."

Until Sara arrived, Lavinia had been Miss Minchin's best-dressed pupil. Now Sara would take her place.

You go at the front, Sara.

The other girls soon adored Sara. She held tea parties in her sitting-room for the younger children, and let them play with her doll, Emily.

11

In the evenings she made up
stories of kings and queens and
beautiful princesses. The others sat
before her and listened, entranced.

Sara had been at Miss Minchin's
school for two years when, one
foggy afternoon, she came back to
her room...

...to find someone asleep in her chair. Looking down, Sara saw it was Becky, the scullery maid.

"Poor thing. She must be exhausted," thought Sara.

At that moment, Becky opened her eyes with a frightened gasp.

"Oh miss! Oh miss!" she stuttered. "I beg yer pardon. It was the warm fire, and me being *so* tired..."

"Don't worry," said Sara, laughing. "You couldn't help it."

Becky stared at Sara. She was used to being ordered about and scolded. She couldn't believe this girl was being kind to her.

"Ain't yer angry, miss?" gasped Becky.

"No," cried Sara, "of course not. We're just the same, you know. I'm only a girl like you. It's just chance that I'm not you and you're not me."

"Would you like to stay a minute?" Sara added. "You could have some cakes."

Becky devoured the cakes in hungry bites, all the time gazing at Sara in wonder. "I think you're like a princess, miss," said Becky.

"I'd love to be a princess!" said Sara. "Perhaps I'll begin pretending I am one. I could think of ways to help people, like real princesses. Will you come and see me again, Becky?"

"Oh yes please," said Becky, and hurried out of the room before Miss Minchin found her.

Chapter 3
Diamond mines

A few weeks later, Sara
received a letter from her father.
It set the whole school talking.

"An old friend has offered me a share in his diamond mines," wrote Captain Crewe. "We'll be rich beyond my wildest dreams. It makes me dizzy to think of it."

Then, shortly before Sara's eleventh birthday, she had another letter from her father. This one sounded quite different.

"I fear your father is not a business man," he wrote. "Each night I lie tossing and turning. I can't sleep for trying to work out the sums. I wish you were here with me."

But despite his worries, Captain Crewe wrote to Miss Minchin, telling her to organize an amazing birthday party for Sara.

Sara was led into the schoolroom by Miss Minchin. Behind her came the servants, carrying boxes overflowing with presents.

"You may leave us," Miss Minchin announced to the servants.

"If you please, Miss Minchin," said Sara, suddenly, "could Becky stay?"

Miss Minchin jumped. "My dear Sara," she said, "Becky is a scullery maid. Scullery maids are not like young ladies."

"But Becky is! Please let her stay... because it's my birthday."

"You are too kind, Sara. Becky, go and stand there," said Miss Minchin, sharply, waving at the door.

The instant Miss Minchin had swept out of the room, everyone rushed to see Sara open her presents. There were books and hats, necklaces and tiaras – but best of all, there was a magnificent doll.

A little while later Miss Amelia popped her head around the schoolroom door. "You're to go for tea, girls. A solicitor has arrived and Miss Minchin wants to talk to him in here."

After the talk, Miss Minchin was in a rage. "Where is Sara Crewe?" she snapped to her sister.

"She's in the tea-room with the others, of course," said Amelia.

"Go and tell her to put on a black dress," ordered Miss Minchin.

"Oh sister!" cried Miss Amelia. "What's happened?"

Miss Minchin wasted no words. "Captain Crewe is dead. He died of jungle fever and..." she added furiously, "he's lost *all* his money."

"*I* paid for this ridiculous party *and* all those presents! I'll never get my money back now," she screamed. "Captain Crewe put all his money into his so-called friend's diamond mine, then the friend disappeared. I'd like to throw Sara out on the street, only it would look bad for the school."

I'll make her work for every penny she owes me.

When Sara came to see Miss Minchin, her face was white and her eyes were red from crying. She held her doll tightly in her arms.

"Put down your doll," ordered Miss Minchin.

"No," Sara answered. "I won't. My father wanted me to have her. She's all I have left of him."

"Everything is different now," said Miss Minchin, growing angry. "You are a beggar, do you understand? You have no relations, no home and no one to take care of you."

Sara's thin, pale face twitched, but she said nothing.

"Don't stare at me like that!" Miss Minchin snapped. "You're going to work for your living now...

You can sleep in the attic, in the room next to Becky. And thank me girl," said Miss Minchin.

"Why should I thank you?"

"For being kind to you, and giving you a home."

"But you're *not* kind," said Sara fiercely. "And this is *not* a home." She turned and ran out of the room, before Miss Minchin could see her cry.

Chapter 4

In the attic

That first night in the attic, Sara lay awake in the dark. She could hear rats scuffling in the walls. "My father's dead!" she sobbed. "I'll never see him again."

Everything in Sara's life changed at once. When she came down the next morning, Lavinia had taken her place next to Miss Minchin.

"You're late, Sara!" said Miss Minchin, coldly. "Don't let it happen again. Begin your new duties by looking after the little ones."

Every day, Sara was sent on
errand after errand. She was
expected to go out in all weathers
and to dust and scrub the rooms.

At the end of each busy day, Miss
Minchin sent her to the schoolroom
to study, so she would learn enough
to teach the younger pupils.

Over time, Sara's frocks grew shorter and shabbier and she became thin and pale. The other pupils stopped talking to her.

"To think she was the girl with the diamond mines," scoffed Lavinia. "Now she's nothing."

"I won't cry," thought Sara, biting hard on her lip. "I won't."

Her only friend was Becky. They had little chance to talk during the day, but each night, Becky crept into Sara's room.

"Let's pretend this room is covered in thick, soft rugs," said Sara. "Over in the corner there's a little sofa, with cushions you can curl up on...

...and a blazing fire."

"Ooh!" said Becky, stretching out her hands. "I can almost feel it, miss."

But once Becky had left, Sara's vision faded from her mind, and the attic was as cold and bare as before. "Sometimes," Sara thought, "it feels like the loneliest place in the world."

Chapter 5

The Magic

One morning, on her way back
from the butcher's, Sara saw that a
van full of furniture had stopped
outside the empty house next door.

"Someone must be moving in," thought Sara. Glancing at the pieces of furniture, she had a weird, homesick feeling. They reminded her of the things they had in India.

"An English gentleman has moved in," Becky told her that night. "He's come from India and his name is Mr. Carrisford. He's rich but he's been very ill."

When Sara next looked out of her window, she heard an odd little squeaky sound coming from the next door attic.

Sara looked over and saw an Indian man-servant – "A Lascar!" she said to herself. He was holding a small chattering monkey.

As the Lascar smiled at her, his hold on the monkey must have loosened. Suddenly, it broke free, ran across the slates, and jumped into Sara's attic.

"Shall I try and catch him?" Sara called to the Lascar.

"No need, Missee Sahib," he answered. "I, Ram Dass, will come and get him."

In no time he had skipped across the rooftops and slipped through her skylight. Ram Dass bowed to Sara, then caught the monkey with ease.

"My master is very fond of this little one," he said, stroking the monkey. He thanked Sara, bowed once more and went back across the rooftops.

"He spoke to me as if I were a princess, not a servant girl," thought Sara. "My clothes might be in rags, but maybe I can still be a princess *inside*."

Meanwhile, in the house next door, Ram Dass was telling his master about the little girl in the attic.

"Poor thing," said Mr. Carrisford. He looked up at his friend. "Do you suppose, Phillips," he said slowly, "that the child I am looking for is living like the little girl next door?"

"No," said Mr. Phillips, soothingly. "I am sure the little girl you are looking for is the one in Paris. And she seems to be in good hands."

"I can't be sure," Mr. Carrisford replied. "After all her name is different. They pronounced it Carew instead of Crewe."

"But the circumstances are so similar," said Mr. Phillips. "An English officer places his motherless little girl in a school, then dies suddenly after losing a fortune."

"You are *sure* the child was left in Paris?" Mr. Phillips went on.

"I am sure of nothing," said Mr. Carrisford. "When I met Ralph Crewe in India, all we spoke of were the diamond mines."

"I must find his daughter! If she is penniless it's my fault. Crewe died thinking I was a villain. If only I hadn't been sick – I could have told him we hadn't lost the money."

"Try not to worry," said Mr. Phillips. "I'll leave for Paris tonight – and I'll find his daughter."

Mr. Carrisford turned to Ram Dass. "In the meantime," he said, "let's do something for the little girl in the attic."

That night, Ram Dass slipped silently into Sara's attic as she slept. He padded noiselessly across the room, weaving his magic...

Sara stirred as her skylight clicked shut. "How strange," she thought. "My room is so warm — and I can actually *feel* blankets. I must be dreaming."

"I don't want to open my eyes," she thought, "or this dream will fade." But it felt so real, she couldn't resist opening them...

...and the dream didn't melt away. There was a blazing fire in her room, blankets and rugs – and a feast laid out on the table. "It's Magic!" thought Sara.

49

There was also a note. "To the little girl in the attic. From a friend." When she saw it, Sara burst into tears.

"Becky! Becky!" Sara whispered as loudly as she dared. "Wake up! Come and see the Magic!"

Chapter 6

The other side of the wall

At the end of each long day, Becky and Sara now climbed their attic stairs to find a fire blazing merrily and plates piled high with food.

Miss Minchin couldn't understand why Sara and Becky were so cheerful.

"Perhaps Sara is a princess after all," suggested Miss Amelia. "How else could she cope so bravely?"

"Don't be ridiculous," snapped Miss Minchin. But she hated seeing Sara so happy.

She's looking almost well-fed.

A few months later, just before Sara went to work, she heard a scratching sound at the skylight. It had been snowing all night, and on the snow, crouched near the skylight, was a tiny, shivering figure.

"Oh it's the monkey from next door!" cried Sara. "I'll coax him in. He can't stay out in the cold."

As Sara was letting in the monkey, Mr. Carrisford was greeting Mr. Phillips in the house next door. He had just returned from Paris.

"It wasn't the child we're looking for," Mr. Phillips said sadly. "Her name was Emily, and she is much younger than Captain Crewe's little girl."

Mr. Carrisford sighed. "Well then," he said, "we must begin our search again at once."

Perhaps the Magic was at work again, for as he spoke Ram Dass came into the room. "Sahib," he said, "the girl from the attic has come. She brings back the monkey."

"Your monkey ran away again," Sara explained. "Shall I give him to the Lascar?"

"How do you know he is a Lascar?" said Mr. Carrisford, smiling a little.

"I was born in India," explained Sara, handing over the monkey.

Mr. Carrisford sat up suddenly. "And now?" he asked. "Now you live next door, but not as a pupil?"

"At first I was a pupil," said Sara. "I was taken there by my Papa. But then he died without any money. And now I sleep in the attic and work for my living."

"How did your father lose his money?" Mr. Phillips broke in breathlessly.

"He had a friend he was very fond of – who took all his money and ran away," said Sara, quietly.

"What was your father's name?" Mr. Carrisford asked. "Tell me."

"His name was Ralph Crewe," Sara answered, feeling startled. "Captain Crewe. He died in India."

"It's her!" gasped Mr. Carrisford. "It's her!"

"What do you mean?" Sara asked.

"I've spent the last two years looking for you," said Mr. Carrisford. "*I* was your father's friend."

"I didn't really lose his money," he went on. "I thought I'd lost it, and that made me ill. But when I was well enough to tell your father, he was already dead."

Sara spoke as if she were in a dream. "And I was at Miss Minchin's all the while," she whispered. "Just on the other side of the wall."

"You need never go back," said Mr. Carrisford, gently. "I'll take care of you now."

Miss Minchin was furious when she found out. "The diamond mines were real after all," she sobbed. "Now I'm not going to see a penny of that money in school fees. *And* Sara's taking Becky with her. I don't deserve this. When I think of all I did for that child..."

For the first time in her life, Miss Amelia spoke her mind to her sister. "You don't deserve any of Sara's money," she said. "It's your fault for being a hard, selfish woman!"

Miss Minchin gasped in shock. And from then on, she began to have a little more respect for her sister.

The next day, Mr. Carrisford took Sara out into the garden. "So Sara," he said. "What are you going to do with your money?"

"I'm going to help people," Sara replied. "Just like a real princess."

Frances Hodgson Burnett was born in Manchester, England, in 1849. After her father's death, the family moved to Tennessee, America, in 1865, where they struggled to earn a living. At 17, Frances sold her first story and she went on to write many novels. Today she is most famous for her children's books, which include *The Secret Garden* and *Little Lord Fauntleroy*.

Series editor: Lesley Sims

Designed by Natacha Goransky

Cover design by Russell Punter

First published in 2005 by Usborne Publishing Ltd., Usborne House, 83-85 Saffron Hill, London EC1N 8RT, England. www.usborne.com
Copyright © 2005 Usborne Publishing Ltd.